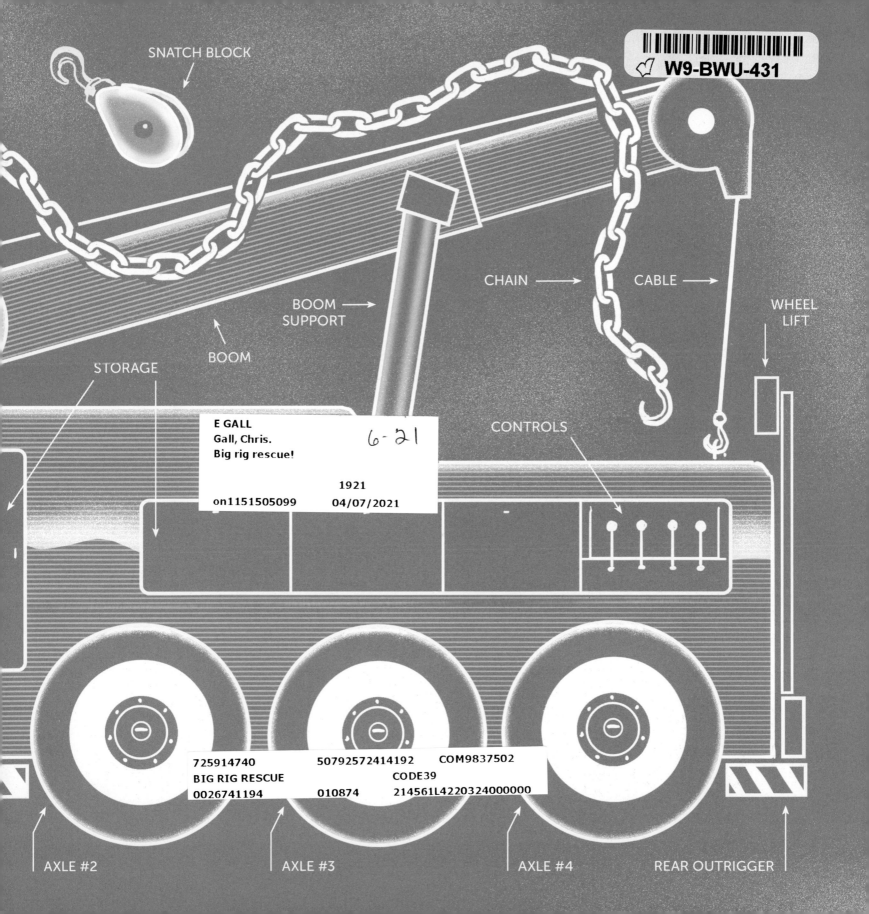

SNATCH BLOCK

W9-BWU-431

CHAIN →   CABLE →

WHEEL
LIFT

BOOM →
SUPPORT

BOOM

STORAGE

CONTROLS

E GALL
Gall, Chris.   6-21
Big rig rescue!

                    1921
on1151505099   04/07/2021

AXLE #2   AXLE #3   AXLE #4   REAR OUTRIGGER

BIG RIG RESCUE!

CHRIS GALL

NORTON YOUNG READERS

An Imprint of W. W. Norton & Company
Independent Publishers Since 1923

For Erica S.

For information about permission to reproduce selections from this book, write to
Permissions, W. W. Norton & Company, Inc., 500 Fifth Avenue, New York, NY 10110

For information about special discounts for bulk purchases, please contact
W. W. Norton Special Sales at specialsales@wwnorton.com or 800-233-4830

Manufacturing by RR Donnelley Shenzhen. Book design by Angela Corbo Gier

Library of Congress Cataloging-in-Publication Data

Names: Gall, Chris, author, illustrator.
Title: Big rig rescue! / Chris Gall.
Description: First edition. | New York, NY : Norton Young Readers, [2021] | Audience: Ages 4–8. |
Summary: When a semi tips over on a mountain road, Big Orange and its driver arrive quickly
with a boom, a winch, and more, but can they pull the truck out before the storm arrives?
Identifiers: LCCN 2020017727 | ISBN 9781324015390 (hardcover) | ISBN 9781324015406 (epub)
Subjects: CYAC: Truck drivers—Fiction. | Wreckers (Vehicles)—Fiction. | Tractor trailers—Fiction. |
Truck accidents—Fiction.
Classification: LCC PZ7.G1352 Big 2021 | DDC [E]—dc23
LC record available at https://lccn.loc.gov/2020017727

W. W. Norton & Company, Inc., 500 Fifth Avenue, New York, N.Y. 10110
www.wwnorton.com

W. W. Norton & Company Ltd., 15 Carlisle Street, London W1D 3BS

1 2 3 4 5 6 7 8 9 0

There's a storm brewing.
And a wreck on the highway!

Big Orange will get there. We've got 14 wheels,
a **boom**, a **hook**, and . . .
Oh yes. A **winch**! Wait 'til you see how that works.

We're here to help, night or day.

We've seen rain.
We've seen mud.
We've seen ice.
And we've seen snow. Lots of snow.

But we've got the power to handle it.

It's haulin' tons of scrap, so it's going to be heavy.
Time to do our job!

Safety first. The driver is OK!

But the truck is leaking gas. A tanker arrives to drain the fuel.

We need to get the semi back on its wheels so we can tow it away.

We're going to need **chains**, some **webbing straps**, and maybe a **snatch block**.

We don't want all that scrap pouring onto the road. What a mess that would be!

The semi is hung up on the guardrail. I'm going to have to do some cutting to get it free.

I love my metal-cutting **rescue saw**.

Zeee

Pump up the **airbags**!
They lift the trailer so we can get some straps underneath it.

Better lower the **outriggers**. They'll keep Big Orange from flipping.

We're going to try to turn the semi over. I pull out the cables and attach the hooks to the straps. Start up the winch.

Let it rip!

Ernnnnhhhhhhh.

The semi isn't budging. We're going to need some help.

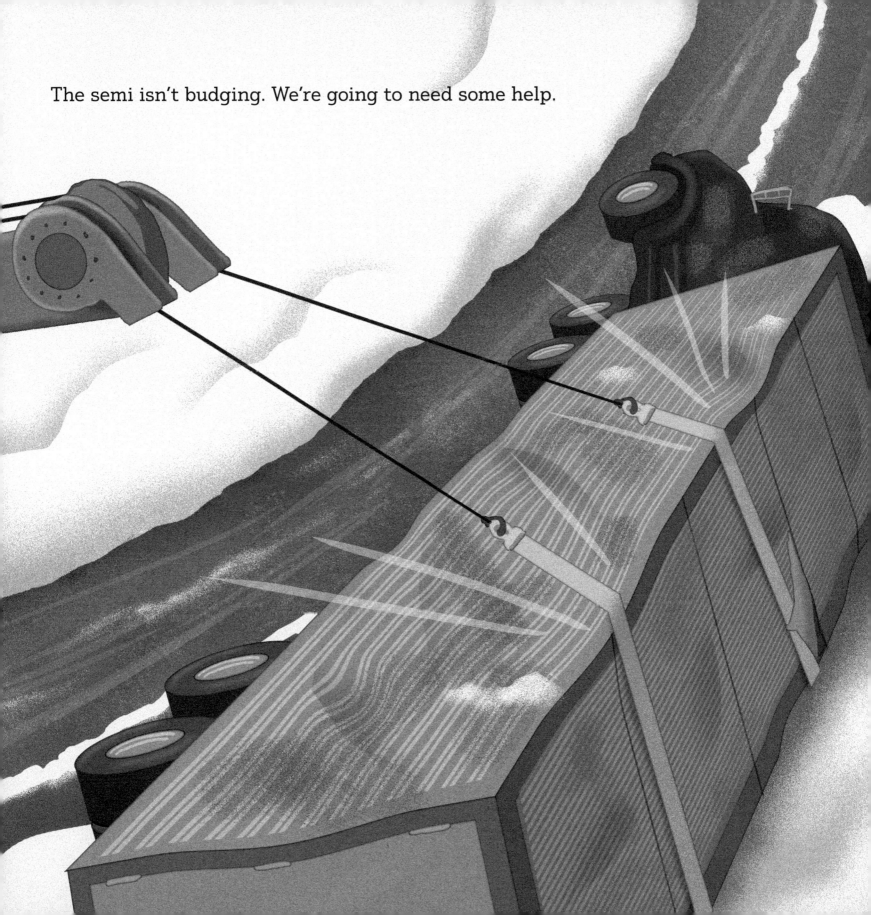

Big Blue is on the way. Now we have a team!

Big Blue attaches a cable and chain to the tractor.
Then we run my line through a snatch block on the trailer
to give us extra power.

Better connect a safety line too! We don't want that semi rolling over on us.

Everybody has to pull at once.
Slowly! Up! Up! Up! Over!

Great roll, everyone!

We all help to lift the trailer onto a flatbed.
Steady! We have to keep that trailer balanced.

Now we get ready for the tow. We'll use hydraulics and the **wheel lift** for that.

Up it goes!

We're off to the repair shop to drop off the tractor. There may be some life in it yet.

All in a day's work!

Uh-oh. Looks like another storm is brewing.

Black ice!

It's a good thing we've got friends!

WEBBING STRAP

EXHAUST STACK

SLEEPER

WINCH

RADIATOR

AIR CLEANER

HEADLIGHT

FUEL TANK

FRONT BUMPER

FRONT OUTRIGGER

FRONT AXLE